W9-BJB-032

ORILLIA PUBLIC LIBRARY

MAY 08 2015

CHILDREN'S DEPARTMENT

Lori Haskins Houran
Illustrated by Francisca Marquez

A TRIP INTO SPACE

SPACE

An Adventure to the International Space Station

FICTION READALONG
AV2 BY WEIGL
AUDIO VISUAL · ADDED VALUE

www.av2books.com

Taking a ride

That starts with a blast

A trip into space

FICTION READALONG
AV2 BY WEIGL™
AUDIO VISUAL · ADDED VALUE

Go to www.av2books.com, and enter this book's unique code.

BOOK CODE

V731695

AV² by Weigl brings you media enhanced books that support active learning.

Follow these steps to access your AV² book.

Step 1
Find the book code above.

Step 2
Enter the code at www.av2books.com.

Step 3
Explore your Fiction Readalong.

First Published by

ALBERT
WHITMAN
& COMPANY
Publishing children's books since 1919

Going to work—
And going there fast!

Whipping through space

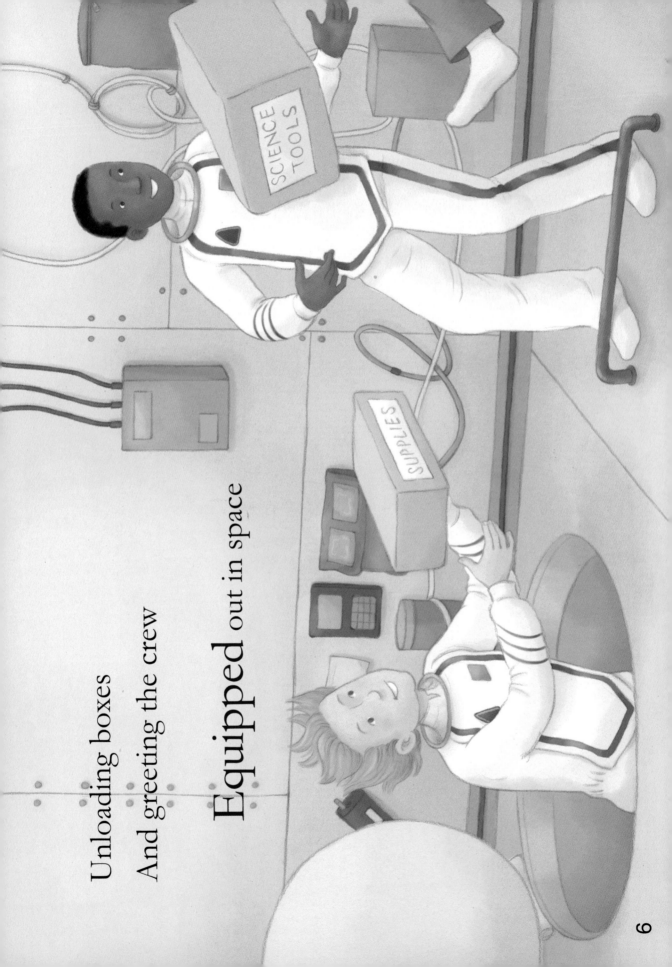

Unloading boxes
And greeting the crew

Equipped out in space

Looking at Earth...

While Earth looks at you...

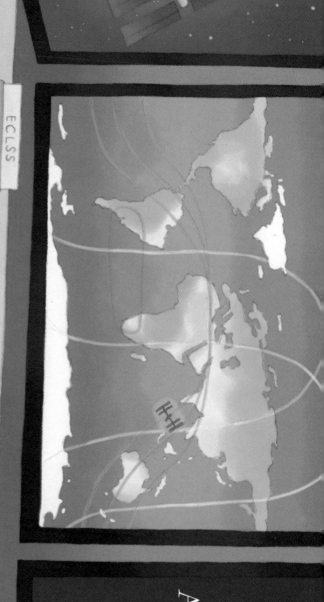

A blip out in space

Tasting a drink
That may float around

12

Sipping in space

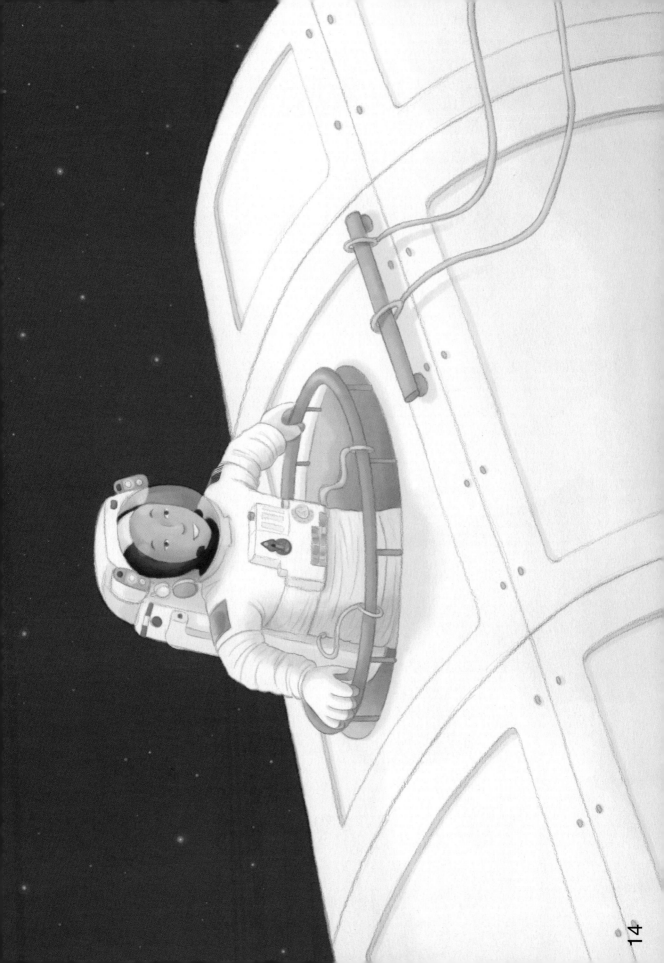

Taking a walk
Without any ground!

Flipping in space

15

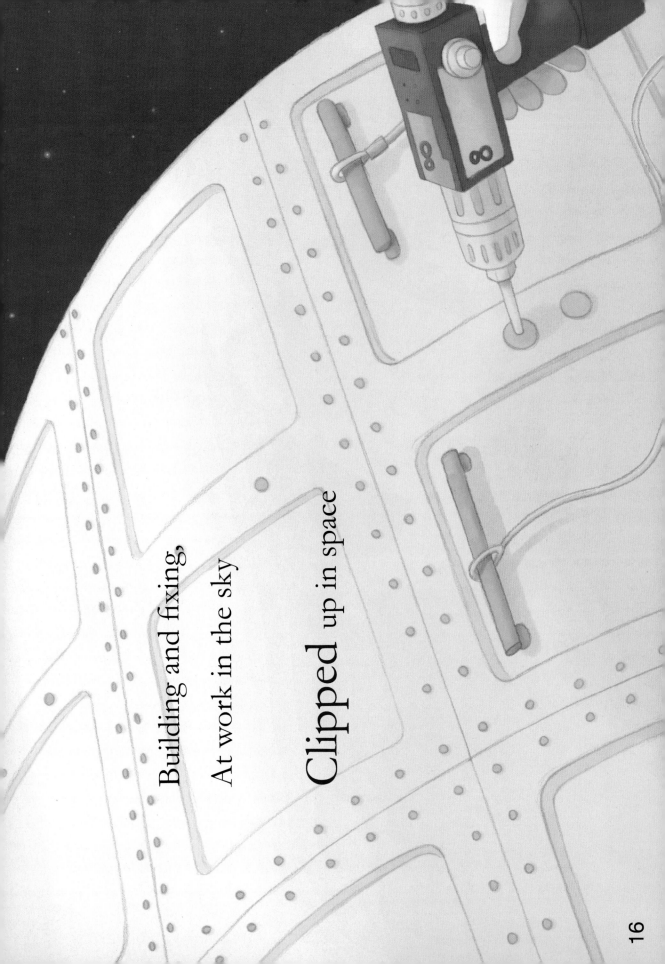

Building and fixing,

At work in the sky

Clipped up in space

Heading for bed—
Two hundred miles high!

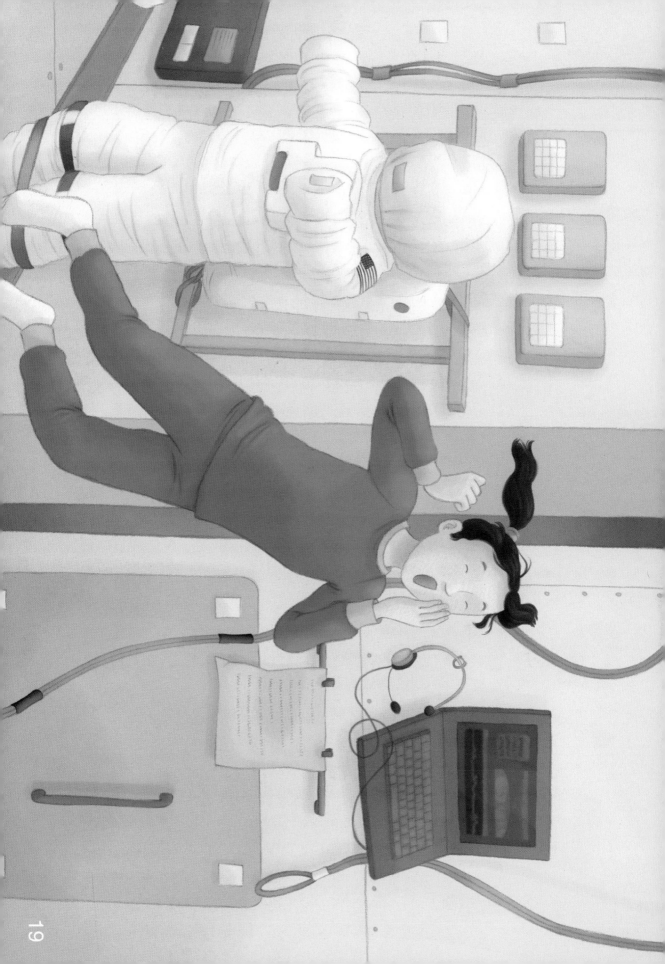

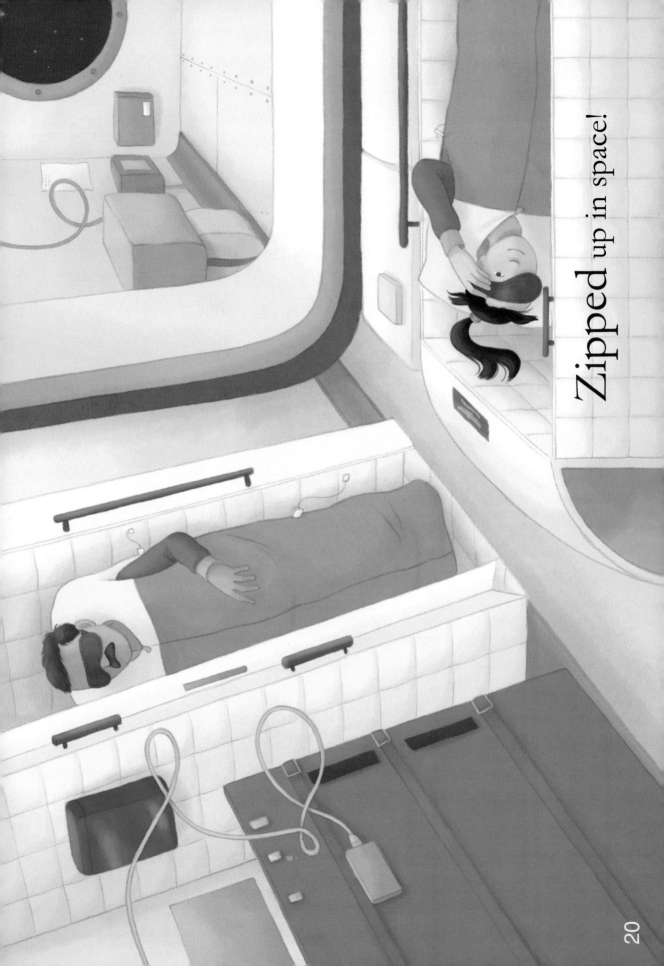

Zipped up in space!

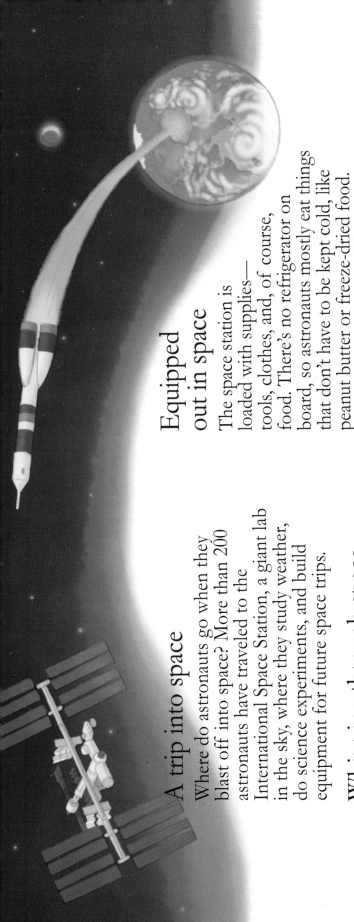

A trip into space

Where do astronauts go when they blast off into space? More than 200 astronauts have traveled to the International Space Station, a giant lab in the sky, where they study weather, do science experiments, and build equipment for future space trips.

Whipping through space

Astronauts travel fast! Their spaceships move up to 17,500 miles per hour. It takes less than six hours to travel from Earth to the space station. That's quicker than an airplane ride from New York to California!

Equipped out in space

The space station is loaded with supplies—tools, clothes, and, of course, food. There's no refrigerator on board, so astronauts mostly eat things that don't have to be kept cold, like peanut butter or freeze-dried food. They love it when new shipments arrive. It's their only chance to eat fresh fruits and veggies!

A blip out in space

The astronauts can see Earth from the space station, and we can see them too. Flight controllers at Mission Control in Houston, Texas, use cameras and computers to watch the station twenty-four hours a day. Some nights, you can look up and see the space station yourself. It appears as a tiny bright light, moving across the sky from west to east.

22

Sipping in space

Gravity is a powerful force that pulls things toward Earth. It keeps your feet on the ground while you're walking around. On the space station, the astronauts can't feel gravity's pull. They don't walk around—they float! Everything else floats too. Even drops of water! That's why the astronauts drink out of pouches instead of regular cups. They also use Velcro to hold down their forks between bites of food.

Flipping in space

Sometimes astronauts go on space walks to do experiments or make repairs outside the space station. The astronauts wear spacesuits that provide air to breathe and water to drink. They wear helmets with visors to protect their eyes from the sun. The visors are lined with real gold!

Clipped up in space

How do astronauts keep from floating off into space during a space walk? They're clipped to the space station with safety tethers. They also have jet packs on their backs that they can use to zoom back to the station if their safety tethers break.

Zipped up in space

Astronauts usually live at the space station for about six months at a time. They eat, work, exercise, and sleep there. To keep from floating around while they rest, the astronauts zip themselves into sleeping bags. Sleep tight!

Your AV² Media Enhanced book gives you a fiction readalong online.
Log on to www.av2books.com and enter the unique book code from
page 2 to use your readalong.

AV² Readalong Navigation

HIGHLIGHTED
TEXT

HOME

CLOSE

TITLE
INFORMATION

PAGE PREVIEW

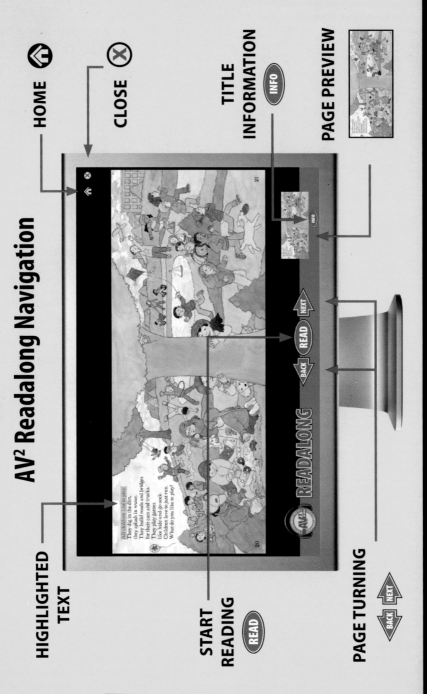

START
READING

PAGE TURNING

Published by AV² by Weigl
350 5ᵗʰ Avenue, 59ᵗʰ Floor New York, NY 10118
Websites: www.av2books.com   www.weigl.com

Printed in the United States of America in North Mankato, Minnesota
1 2 3 4 5 6 7 8 9 0 18 17 16 15 14

042014
WEP080414

Library of Congress Control Number: 2014938424

ISBN 978-1-4896-2837-4 (hardcover)
ISBN 978-1-4896-2838-1 (single user eBook)
ISBN 978-1-4896-2839-8 (multi-user eBook)

Copyright ©2015 AV² by Weigl
All rights reserved. No part of this publication may be reproduced,
stored in a retrieval system, or transmitted in any form or by any means,
electronic, mechanical, photocopying, recording, or otherwise, without
the prior written permission of the publisher.

Text copyright ©2014 by Lori Haskins Houran.
Illustrations copyright ©2014 by Albert Whitman & Company.
Published in 2014 by Albert Whitman & Company.

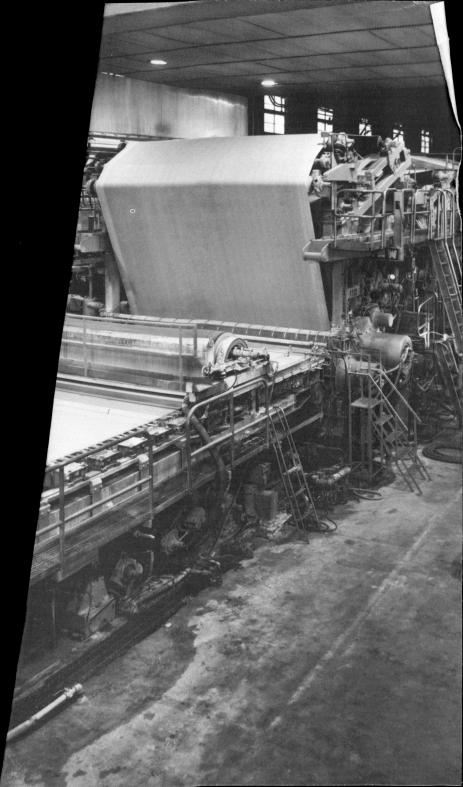

PA

PAPER

INVENTIONS THAT CHANGED OUR LIVES

By Elizabeth Simpson Smith

E.C.I.A. CHAPTER 2

9/2.77

12-18-89

BRAZOS
MIDDLE SCHOOL
LIBRARY

WALLIS ELEMENTARY SCHOOL

8225

WALKER AND COMPANY New York

Library of Congress Cataloging in Publication Data

Smith, Elizabeth Simpson.
   Paper.

   (Inventions that changed our lives)
   Includes index.
   Summary: Presents the history and evolution of papermaking,
introducing the people and processes involved.
   1. Paper—Juvenile literature. [1. Paper—History. 2. Paper
making and trade—History] I. Title. II. Series.
TS1105.5.S65 1984   676'.09   84-7271
ISBN 0-8027-6543-2

Copyright © 1984 by Elizabeth Simpson Smith

All rights reserved. No part of this book may be reproduced or transmitted in any form or by any means, electric or mechanical, including
photocopying, recording, or by any information storage and retrieval
system, without permission in writing from the Publisher.

First published in the United States of America in 1984 by the Walker
Publishing Company, Inc.

Published simultaneously in Canada by John Wiley & Sons Canada,
Limited, Rexdale, Ontario.

Book design by Lena Fong Hor

This edition printed in 1986.

Printed in the United States of America

10 9 8 7 6 5 4 3 2

FOR MY NEPHEWS
Carl, III
Bobby
Richard
Stephen
Lester
Nicky, Jr.
Teddy
Benjamin
and for Greg

ACKNOWLEDGMENTS

In addition to the contributors of photographs and illustrations mentioned elsewhere in this book, the author expresses grateful appreciation to the following for their help: M. M. Matthews, Tom Cox, Robert Morrell, Faye Meek, Teddy Smith, W. A. Weaver, American Forest Institute, Kimberly-Clark Corporation, American Paper Institute, U.S. Forest Service, Westvaco Corporation, S. D. Warren Company, Olin Corporation's Ecusta Paper and Film Group, Champion International Corporation, Gutta Works Company, The Paper Publications Society of Amsterdam, North Western Museum of Science & Industry, Y. K. Yung and most especially to Ed Smith.

CONTENTS

Popular products made of paper (*Forest Products Laboratory*) Forest
Service, U.S. Department of Agriculture

Preface

THIS MORNING you woke up to a world so blessed with paper that it has become commonplace. Before your day was an hour old you came in contact with paper a dozen times — or more.

The wall beside your bed may be covered with paper. Your lamp may wear a paper shade. You used paper tissue in the bathroom. Your soap, toothbrush and toothpaste all came housed in paper. Your breakfast cereal flowed from a paper box. You topped it with milk from a paper carton. Your eggs, bread and butter, even your salt and pepper, were packaged in paper. You probably used a paper napkin, and if there was a spill — or a sneeze — you grabbed for a paper towel or tissue. All within a single hour!

As the day progressed you continued to use

Paper packaging is practical and efficient (*Sonoco Products Company*)

paper in different forms — newspapers, writing paper, shoe boxes, telephone book, school supplies, drinking straws, loudspeakers, even a postage stamp.

And now you're reading a book made of paper!

In fact, as an individual you will use between 600 and 1,000 pounds of paper this year — and probably more next year. There are more than 100,000 uses for paper today, so many that we are said to live in a "paper society." Although many of the products we use are not made of paper — such as furniture,

Paper floats in weightless environment aboard a space ship
(*Courtesy NASA*)

bicycles or automobiles — they were first designed on paper and produced in factories that would find it difficult to exist without the use of paper. There is hardly a product that doesn't use paper at some stage of its manufacture, shipment or sale. To build a large ship, for instance, requires about 100 tons of paper in blueprints, contracts, writing paper, packaging and construction. Our new technological age, with its computer printouts and faster methods of communication, will demand even more paper.

Paper manufacturing is this nation's oldest

Astronaut John W. Young's flight data is recorded on paper aboard the Columbia *(Courtesy NASA)*

industry. The United States is the largest user of paper in the world—if the logs used to make paper for one year in this country alone were laid end to end, the line would reach beyond the moon!

Few products today are as versatile as paper. It can be cut, twisted, glued, stapled, painted and molded. It can be made delicate enough for Bible pages or strong enough for roofing. It can be soft enough to clean eyeglasses, or tough enough for underground meter boxes. It can be pretty enough for gift wrappings, or durable enough for table tops. It can serve as shoe insoles or walls of buildings. It can be safe enough to preserve food products for years, and dependable enough for use in surgery.

Yet, despite its many uses and forms, paper is actually a simple product. If you tear the corner off a fairly thick piece of paper, such as a theater ticket or matchbook cover, and stroke the edges between your thumb and forefinger, you will soon notice a fringe of tiny hairlike fibers. That, basically, is what constitutes paper — organic fibers that have been separated until each fiber stands alone, mixed with water until the fibers become porous, then matted

Grocery shopping includes many paper products (*Scott Paper Company*)

Throwaway non-woven paper gowns are used in hospitals and doctors' offices (*American Threshold Industries*)

together, or intertwined, into a flat sheet. This sheet of intertwined fibers is called *true paper*.

If you'd like to examine paper more thoroughly, take a sheet of notebook paper and tug at it in different directions. You will notice that the sheet is stronger in one direction. This is the direction in which the papermaking machine was traveling because the greatest number of fibers lies in that course. Thus, if you tear the paper you will observe more resistance in the cross-machine direction because you are tearing against the largest number of fibers.

Most paper today is made by high-speed automated machines that perform miracles before your eyes. But when paper first came into existence it was made by hand in a long, laborious process. Unlike today, only royalty or very rich people ever saw a piece of paper. But oddly enough, despite all the sophistication of today's machinery, the process of papermaking remains basically unchanged since paper's invention 2,000 years ago.

Historians and scholars still do not agree as to just who the inventor of paper was. But they do agree that the inventor could never have foreseen the multi-billion-dollar business his invention triggered. Nor could he have envisioned its many uses. For paper was invented for one purpose only — that of communication.

1

The Invention of
Paper

EVER SINCE THE BEGINNING of history, man
has been trying to find ways to communicate his
thoughts and ideas. Cave dwellers drew simple fig-
ures on the walls of their caves. Later civilizations
used a stylus, a sharply pointed writing instrument,
to carve letters into wet clay tablets or scratch them
into metal. Sometimes the tablets were coated with
wax so they could be erased and used again. Notes
were also scratched into stones, shards of broken
pottery, tree bark and leaves.

All of this required great effort and much time,
and even then the results were not very satisfactory.
Clay tablets were heavy and difficult to transport.
Pottery was easily shattered, and stones apt to be
misplaced or lost. Tree bark and leaves dis-

integrated and the messages rotted away.

Some civilizations used parchment made from sheepskin, or vellum made from the skin of calves, goats or lambs. The skins were split, dried, scraped, chalked and pumiced until their surfaces became smooth. Then they were used as pages for messages written with pen and ink, mostly religious writings recorded in monasteries by monks with lots of time on their hands.

The first major breakthrough in a writing material occurred about 2400 B.C. with the development of papyrus in Egypt. Papyrus, a reed native to the banks of the Nile River, sometimes grew stems as thick as a man's wrist. The pith, or soft center, of the stem could be pressed and layered into sheets for writing. The writing material, like the reed, is called papyrus. Also from this word comes the name *paper*, but the name is misleading. Since the fibers of the pith are never separated, moistened and intertwined, papyrus is not *true paper* as we know it today. But papyrus was by far the best writing material available and its use spread to Greece and Rome.

Then in 250 B.C. a Chinese man of learning, Mêng Tien, invented a brush made of camel's hair, and the Chinese began using the brush to write on bamboo strips or on woven cloth, mostly silk. The Chinese characters, however, were delicately drawn or painted and the Chinese soon discovered they needed a smoother surface on which to work. From this great need grew the invention of paper.

Although there is no conclusive proof for the true inventor of paper, the most common story is that Ts'ai Lun, an official in the court of Emperor Ho-Ti at Lei-Yang in the Hunan Province of China, made the first paper in the year 105 A.D. Other stories report that paper was made many years before and that Ts'ai Lun merely used the information gleaned from the earlier efforts. But even if Ts'ai Lun did not make the first paper, he was responsible for officially introducing it and for advancing the art of papermaking to a remarkable degree.

Ts'ai Lun was born a peasant. As a child he was castrated and made to serve as a eunuch in the court of the emperor for the rest of his days. These court eunuchs were supervised by Queen Dun-Shi, herself a great and renowned scholar. Even before she became queen she studied all day and long into the evening, reading classics written on scrolls of silk. After she was elevated to Noble Lady of the court, Dun-Shi refused the jewels and fancy dresses that most Noble Ladies received. Instead she asked for silk papers for writing. And when she was raised to queen in 102 A.D., her first command was to forbid gifts of gold, gems or jewels from the princes and declared that the only gift acceptable to her would be silk paper. Dun-Shi, it is said, is the only queen in the history of China to turn her back on the adornments that most queens cherish.

Because the silk writing paper she desired was

so scarce, Dun-Shi ordered Ts'ai Lun, known throughout the court for his cleverness, to create a cheaper and more abundant writing material.

Ts'ai Lun worked diligently at the project, trying all the native materials available to him. Time after time he failed, and time after time he began anew. The other eunuchs worked only five days, then took a holiday to rest. But Ts'ai Lun worked straight through the week, stopping only to eat and sleep. After more than 16 years of effort, he finally developed a formula that excited him.

Ts'ai Lun carefully shredded the bark from a mulberry tree, mixed it with scraps of linen and with hemp from fishing nets, soaked the mixture in a large vat of water until it became soggy, then beat it with blunt implements until the fibers fell apart and formed a pulp. He dipped a mold, made of loosely woven cloth stretched over a bamboo frame, into the vat and scooped up the pulp. Gently he tilted the mold backwards and forwards and from side to side to spread the pulp evenly. When most of the water had drained through the cloth, Ts'ai Lun laid the mold in the sun to dry.

And the result, at last, was a large sheet of *true paper*!

Although Ts'ai Lun would not have described it in these words, the natural organic fibers from the mulberry tree, the linen and the hemp had separated into unconnected units, then had formed bonds through their hydrogen ions and had interlocked

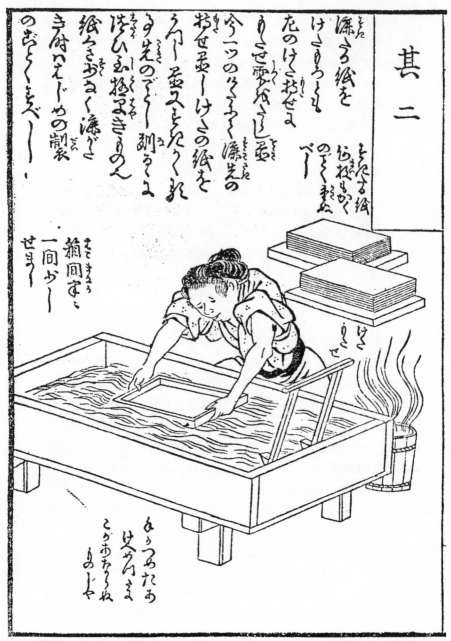

Eighteenth century Japanese illustration of papermaking
using the Chinese method

into a continuous mass. This is still the basic process for making *true paper*, although the product today is called simply paper.

Ts'ai Lun joyfully announced his findings to the court. He was promptly elevated to a higher position, held in esteem for the rest of his life and, to this day, his name is revered. This single act is said to have set off mankind's greatest revolution in communications.

At first the knowledge of papermaking remained a carefully guarded secret known only within China. Because of paper, Chinese culture progressed faster than any other culture in the world. Books were written by scribes, emperors collected them for their libraries, and members of their courts attained a level of education not found in other countries.

The kings and queens of Europe, meanwhile, could not read or even write their own names!

During this period, however, China was engaged in an active silk trade with the west. Camel caravans snaking across the old silk routes through Turkestan, Persia and Syria gradually carried the news of paper with them, no doubt smuggling some of it across the border. By the end of the fifth century paper of some form was in use in large portions of Asia.

Then in 751 A.D. an Arab army made a swift raid into China. Among the captives they whisked away from Samarkand (then in China, now in Rus-

Model of a German paper mill in the year 1700 (*The Dard Hunter Paper Museum*)

sia) were two experienced papermakers. In exchange for their freedom, the papermakers revealed their secret knowledge and opened the doors of culture to the rest of the world.

The skill spread slowly westward to Damascus, to Egypt and finally to Europe. The first European paper mill was established in Sativa, Spain, in 1151, more than 1,000 years after Ts'ai Lun spread his molds to dry in a sunny courtyard on the opposite side of the world.

From Europe papermaking eventually traveled across the ocean to the New World. Although there

Model showing interior view of a German paper mill in the
year 1700 (*The Dard Hunter Paper Museum*)

was a kind of paper made in Latin America before
the European method was introduced, it was not a
true paper. The Mayas and Aztecs made a writing
material by beating flat the bark of fig and mulberry
trees and using it for their hieroglyphic charts. Some
natives in the South Sea Islands had made a similar
substance about 500 A.D., but again this substance
was not true paper since the fibers were merely
beaten flat and not intertwined. The resulting paper
was not satisfactory and the craft did not spread.

The first mill for true paper in the New World
was established in Culhuacan near Mexico City

The Rittenhouse Mill the first paper mill established in the colonies (*The Historical Society of Pennsylvania*)

sometime at the end of the fifteenth century. By 1690, the colonies in North America had their first paper mill. William Rittenhouse, a German who had learned the craft before coming to America, joined with a group of influential citizens from Germantown, Pennsylvania, to build a mill on the banks of the Wissahickon Creek nearby. And so papermaking became the colonies' first industry!

The Rittenhouse mill grew famous throughout the colonies and did a brisk business until 1701, when it was swept away by a flood. A year later the mill was rebuilt on the same site.

In 1710 William DeWees, a Rittenhouse relative by marriage, established another mill in the same area. And nearly twenty years later, in 1729, the Ivy Mill was built on Chester Creek near

Philadelphia by Thomas Willcox, an English emigrant and a close friend of Benjamin Franklin. The mill became a training ground for papermakers so they could establish mills in other areas. Franklin provided money and credit to set up the new plants and helped the owners find supplies and good craftsmen.

Early papermakers, in fact, had a great friend and ally in Benjamin Franklin. Franklin not only used great quantities of paper in his own printing and publishing business, giving the new mills large orders to fill, but he encouraged them to persevere in their efforts to build up the fledgling industry. He had traveled and lived abroad and knew the importance that paper had assumed in Europe. Like other leaders of the day, he was convinced that without paper the colonies could not flourish. Without it, most of the settlers would never learn to read and write. Schools were few and scattered, and their students had only slates or slabs of wood on which to learn. Without education there would be no communication except by word of mouth, and any attempt at commerce would be doomed to failure.

Although the colonists were proud of their first industry and optimistic about its future, they had some major problems to tackle. Paper was still being made by a slow hand process. It remained a precious commodity, extremely expensive and available only to the upper classes. The mills could supply only a portion of the demand for paper, and the settlers continued to look to England for imports.

But even more alarming was a severe shortage of organic fibers for pulp. Although the Chinese method of papermaking was now known throughout the civilized world, one important ingredient had been left out. The Chinese had used mulberry bark for their basic raw material, but this part of their secret was lost to the western world for almost 2,000 years!

2

The Great Rag Need

WITHOUT THE KNOWLEDGE of the mulberry bark, the papermakers in Europe and America used rags of linen and cotton for their organic fibers. The rags were wetted and allowed to mildew or rot so the fibers would break apart. The rotted rags were then boiled in ashes to break down the fibers even more. After that they were washed and cleaned, then beaten into pulp either by hand or with crude devices.

The process was long and arduous. At least a third of the rags wasted away and there was never enough to supply the industry.

Yet another problem for the papermaker was the growing use of the printing press, first developed by Johannes Gutenberg in the middle of the fifteenth century. Books had become available to the

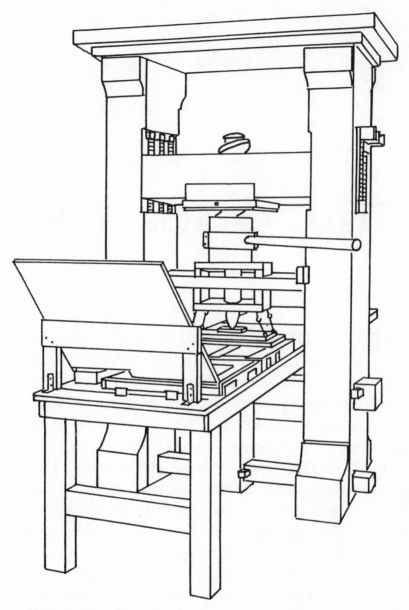

Replica of the Gutenberg press (*illustration by Ward Nichols, courtesy of The Printing Industry of the Carolinas, Inc.*)

common masses. Printing presses continued to spring to life all across Europe, each one gobbling up more and more paper. And the rag shortage became alarming.

Each country had dealt with the problem in any manner it could find. Some passed laws forbidding the export of rags, but this set off a rash of smuggling. Germany decreed that dead bodies be wrapped in wool instead of the customary linen and cotton. England followed suit. And early in the seventeenth century, the lawmakers of London, suspecting that the deadly black plague was being spread by rags, ordered that all rags be burned. This act all but closed the London paper mills for more than a year.

The problem still existed a century later, and in America advertising campaigns were launched. One newspaper ad read:

Kind friend, when thy old shirt is rent,
Let it to the paper mill be sent.

Another ad begged housewives to make a rag-bag and hang it under the family Bible for collecting scraps. Still other ads offered ribbons, thimbles, rings, beads or knives in exchange for rags. Tin peddlers, who normally drove carts throughout the countryside to sell household goods, now traded their goods for rags instead of money. For a while the farm women were delighted to get a brand new cooking pot or a pair of beads for a pile of worn-out clothing. But then they, too, suffered a shortage in their households, for to spin yarn and weave cloth in the home took long, tedious hours. So they added another patch to the garment instead of tossing it in the rag-bag.

During the American Revolution paper was so scarce that General George Washington discharged papermakers from the army and sent them home so they could make paper. Washington and his officers had to write their important messages on any scrap of paper they could find, while their soldiers ripped pages from books to make wadding for their guns.

It is said that during the Civil War some paper mill executives were so hard put for rags that they imported mummies from Egypt, ripped off the cloth they were wrapped in and used it to make pulp.

Papermakers on both sides of the ocean frantically experimented with a host of other materials to replace rags. They tried tree moss, sugarcane, grapevine bark, potato skins, cabbage stalks, Indian corn and straw. Some even tried okra stems. But nothing worked as well as rags. What they desperately needed was a material that would be plentiful, inexpensive and in constant supply. Ironically they were surrounded by the perfect material the whole time they were searching. In fact, the material was so obvious that they had entirely overlooked it.

It took an insect to lead them to it.

Early in the eighteenth century a French scientist, René-Antoine Ferchault de Réaumur, was out walking in the woods when he discovered an empty

Gutenberg's first Bible was printed on vellum (*The Printing Industry of the Carolinas, Inc.*)

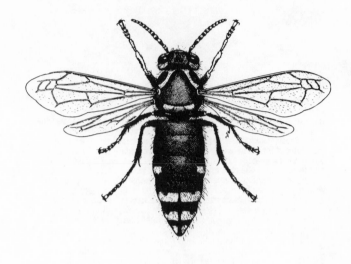

A wasp

wasp nest. Since he was an entomologist (a student of insects) he paused to examine it. And what he found astounded him.

The nest was made of a crude form of paper!

Aware of the world's great need for paper, he became amused that a mere insect was able to manufacture it, apparently with ease. And then he grew perplexed. How could an insect secure rags for making paper? There were no rags in the forest. As he puzzled he became more and more intrigued. And finally he was sure he had the answer.

The wasp, since it lived in the woods, must have used trees.

Réaumur set about to observe the wasp and to study its digestive organs. He discovered that a wasp will scrape wood from trees, produce a powder with the scrapings, mix the powder with its own digestive juices, and transform this pulp into thin layers of grey paper. And from this paper the wasp constructs a nest that houses whole colonies of insects and lasts for years and years.

On November 15, 1719, Réaumur announced his findings to the French Academy. He said, in part, "The wasps . . . invite us to try whether we cannot make fine and good paper from the use of certain woods."

Football-shaped nest is made of paper

But the French Academy, and indeed the world, paid him little attention, and papermakers continued to plod along with their rag pulp. In 1880, about 80 years after Réaumur made his announcement, an Englishman by the name of Matthias Koops published a book, part of which was printed on paper made of wood pulp. But again the paper industry turned its back, and Koops eventually went bankrupt trying to win acceptance for a new process.

In 1839 Charles Fenerty, a Canadian youth, began building a machine that would chafe wood into a pulp much the way that a wasp digests wood fibers. After five years of toil he succeeded in making one sheet of paper from the pulp. His machine worked, but it obviously was not very efficient.

But during the same year, 1844, a German weaver patented a wood-grinding machine that was both practical and efficient. Friedrich Gottlob Keller got the idea while watching small children make beads from cherry pits. In order to flatten and polish the pits, the youngsters secured them on a notched block of wood and rubbed them against a grindstone. Keller noticed that the friction caused wood fibers to fall away where the block rubbed against the stone. Picking up the fibers, he found they were moist and that they matted together in layers, just as the rag fibers did in papermaking. Their cellulose, the fibrous part of the cell wall, combined naturally with lignin, a glue-like substance found within the bark, to form the perfect pulp for papermaking. Wood was plentiful, it was inexpensive and there was a constant supply.

At last, after 19 centuries of papermaking, humans began using a raw material that a tiny creature of nature had used instinctively all along.

3

Papermaking Goes Mechanical

ALTHOUGH PAPER MILLS sprang up like mushrooms in Europe and America, only a few improvements were made over Ts'ai Lun's manner of manufacture. Papermakers devised means of speeding up production and reducing manpower by creating crude contraptions and by using waterwheels, windmills and draft animals as sources of power. The Hollander beater, for instance, was developed in the Netherlands during the seventeenth century. Powered by a windmill, the beater used blades inside a circular tub to grind the pulp. The principle behind the Hollander beater is still in use today.

But the actual art of turning pulp into paper remained a hand process. Craftsmen continued to plod along, dipping the pulp, draining off the water, smoothing, pressing and drying each sheet. Today a modern machine can produce 2,000 feet per minute, and the paper will be 20 feet wide. But then one highly skilled papermaker might turn out only 750 sheets in one good day, and the sheets would be the size of a small page.

In 1798 a young office clerk in a paper mill in Essonne, France, listened to the constant bickering among the other workers and grew impatient. Making paper required so many workers that they seemed to step on one another. Nicholas-Louis Robert could hardly think straight enough to get his own work done. What the paper industry needed, he knew, was a machine that would relieve some of the work load and reduce the number of workers.

With the permission of Léger Didot, owner of the mill, Robert spent his spare time trying to invent such a machine. The device he came up with was simple and crude but it set off a chain reaction that eventually resulted in today's high speed machinery. Robert's contraption consisted of a vat, a paddle wheel, a rotating belt of wire mesh and a press, all run by a waterwheel. The machine dumped the liquid pulp onto a wire screen, thus saving the dipping process. But Robert's first device proved to be a failure. Later, however, an improved version was so successful that the French government awarded him 3,000 francs.

His employer, unfortunately, became disgruntled when Robert applied for a patent, and

Model of the first paper machine *(The Dard Hunter Paper Museum)*

hauled him into court. Robert won the case but, in a burst of generosity, signed over his rights to Didot. Robert lost his job, had to return to teaching and later died penniless.

Conditions in France, meanwhile, were very unsettled and Didot feared for the future of his machine. To secure its safety he moved it to England in 1801, where he gained the financial help of Henry and Sealy Fourdrinier, two brothers engaged in papermaking. Pooling their resources, Didot and the Fourdrinier brothers hired Bryan Donkin, a gifted

38

engineer, to build a new and improved machine patterned after Robert's.

Within two years Donkin had his device running smoothly at Frogmore Mill in Hertfordshire, England. Four years later an improved version was ready for marketing. The first paper machine set up in America was one built by Donkin in England and shipped to Henry Barclay's mill in Saugerties, New York, in 1827.

Although the machine revolutionized papermaking, most of the men involved in its invention met with ill fortune. Only Donkin gained any wealth. Didot and the Fourdrinier brothers, like Nicholas-Louis Robert, went bankrupt. But the Fourdrinier brothers at least were recognized for their contribution. Today the papermaking machine is still called a fourdrinier (pronounced four-dri-NEER).

If you visit a paper mill (many of them offer tours), you will notice that it is located on the bank of a river or large lake, with water treatment and waste disposal plants nearby. Papermakers use vast quantities of water, for 175 gallons of liquid are needed to make a single pound of paper. The paper industry in the United States alone uses about 6 trillion gallons of water each day, enough to supply the daily needs of 6,000 cities the size of New York. The water is recycled time after time and is carefully purified before it is returned to its source.

When you enter a plant you will be given ear

Water plays a major role in papermaking *(Sonoco Products Company)*

plugs and protective eyeglasses to wear, for the machinery is both loud and swift and paper manufacturers are safety-conscious. As you move from operation to operation you will soon be struck by the fact that paper today is manufactured the same way that Ts'ai Lun made his first sheet. Automated machinery now does the work that hands once performed, but the process remains the same.

Paper manufacturing is generally divided into three processes or stages — pulping, papermaking and converting. Pulping transforms organic raw material into pulp, papermaking then turns the pulp into paper, and the converting process converts the paper into usable products.

Sometimes all three operations are owned by one large company and are spread out in a sprawling complex of buildings, all located at one site. Often, however, the plants are in separate locations, sometimes even in different cities.

Strong, thin paper for Bible pages or cigarette paper is made from seed flax grown in the Dakotas, Minnesota and Southern Canada. And some fine paper is made from rags. But more than 95 percent of the pulp used today is made from logs, so paper manufacturing really begins in the forest.

Most of the major paper manufacturers own huge tracts of woodlands where they grow and harvest their own trees. The paper industry takes great pains to prevent depleting these forests. Because it takes only 12 to 30 years to grow a tree suitable for papermaking, trees are called a "renewable resource." The forests are regularly reseeded and a new crop is always in the making. In the meantime, they can be enjoyed for their beauty and used for wildlife and recreation.

Much of the wood for papermaking, however, is grown by individual landowners and bought by the manufacturers. Four million private citizens of the United States own about 60 percent of the nation's commercial forests. These people are called tree farmers and their woodlands are called tree farms. The paper industry often sponsors programs to teach

One machine can plant up to 10,000 seedlings a day (*International Paper Company*)

good forest management to these tree farmers to help them improve their properties and the quality of their trees.

At first only softwoods, such as pine and spruce, were used for pulp because they have longer fibers and produce stronger paper. But improved methods of manufacture now make it possible to use hardwoods, such as oak, maple, elm, ash and birch. And with today's technology, mills can now use parts of the forest that were formerly wasted — slabs and edgings of trees, branches and even roots — so very little has to be destroyed. The paper industry is also careful to recycle all unused components during the manufacture. Leftover pulp, scraps of paper, chemicals and water are run back through the system again and again.

After the trees are felled and cut into four- to eight-foot lengths, the logs are transported to the pulp mill by truck, railroad cars or by floating them down rivers and lakes. At the pulp mill they are washed to remove dirt and foreign matter. Then the bark is removed by either tumbling the logs in rotating cylinders or by using high pressure water sprays to lift off the bark. The logs are then ready for pulping.

There are generally two methods of pulping: mechanical and chemical. In mechanical pulping the logs are fed sideways into large grinding wheels. The resulting pulp is called groundwood and is used for non-permanent purposes, such as newspapers,

Trees are cut into logs
(*Georgia-Pacific Corporation*)

Logs are shipped by truck and rail to the pulp mill (*Wisconsin Paper Council*)

magazines and paper toweling, all of which are usually discarded.

For chemical pulp, logs are cut into three-quarter-inch chips by feeding them into rotating discs equipped with knives. Then the chips are chemically cooked in a digester, or large tank, for two to twelve hours at a temperature over 300 degrees Fahrenheit. Except for size, the digester resembles a kitchen pressure cooker. It can reach five stories tall and stretch 18 feet in diameter. During the cooking process the lignin, a natural binding found within logs, is removed. Lignin holds the fibers of a tree together but when left in the pulp it causes the paper to turn yellow. It is therefore not suitable for paper that is not to be thrown away.

Wood chips are stacked in
huge piles outside a paper
mill (*Georgia-Pacific Corporation*)

After the chemical cooking the pulp ends up a
brown, soggy mass. It is then strained to remove
lumps, bleached if the paper is to be white and ends
up looking like cooked oatmeal, perhaps a little
soupier than the breakfast variety. This is called
slurry.

The slurry flows through pipes and troughs and
next undergoes a mechanical beating. The beating
roughens the surface of the fibers so they will lock
together more firmly and make a stronger paper.

The mixture, now 99.5 percent water and .5 percent pulp, is ready to be made into paper on the
fourdrinier machine. These machines are often
longer than a football field or a city block, and perform their magic at high speeds. The mixture of pulp

A vat of slurry (*Hammermill Paper Company*)

and water is poured onto an endless wire screen traveling around and around at speeds up to 30 miles per hour. As the screen surges forward it shakes the pulp from side to side, just as Ts'ai Lun did, and spreads it out evenly. Meanwhile, water drains through the screen, leaving a very wet sheet. This sheet is squeezed even drier when it is run between rollers and over steam-heated cylinders until the remaining moisture is only about five percent, the standard for paper. The pressure of the rollers has also matted together, or intertwined, the tiny fibers, thereby locking them securely. The endless screen meanwhile loops back underneath the

A paper machine can be as long as a football field (*Hammermill Paper Company*)

Steel calender rolls give paper a smooth finish (*Hammermill Paper Company*)

Paper is being wound onto a roll (*Georgia-Pacific Corporation*)

machine and around again, continuously picking up fresh pulp and turning it into one long, ongoing sheet.

The paper is ironed smooth when run through a series of rollers, called calender stacks, and finally wound into rolls. The finished rolls can be 8 feet in diameter and more than 20 feet, or two stories, tall.

Papermakers are able to produce many different types of paper by making variations in any of the steps of manufacture, such as changing the type of wood, the cooking time or temperature, the degree of beating or the water content. During the process paper can be coated with clay, calcium carbonate,

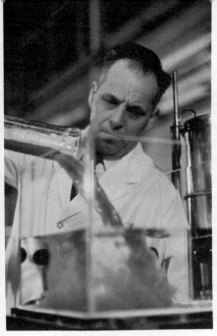

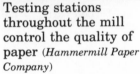

Testing stations
throughout the mill
control the quality of
paper (*Hammermill Paper
Company*)

Modern computers control
the machines (*Wisconsin Paper
Council*)

titanium dioxide or with waterproofing material such as wax and polyethylene to suit the end use. Dyes may also be added along the way.

Depending on the formula, the finished paper may be thin and transparent, thick and opaque, flexible as a handkerchief or rigid as steel, soft or hard, smooth as a marble or rough as sandpaper. Along the way the paper is carefully checked at various stages by highly qualified inspectors. The formulas are worked out on computers and the machines are run automatically. But the final control rests with the skilled worker, who can tell by touch or sight if the product is exactly the way it should be.

Oven trays now can be specially treated for use in both microwave and conventional ovens (*International Paper Company*)

This new package for juice need not be refrigerated until opened (*International Paper Company*)

Women sense it immediately

—that atmosphere of elegance and refinement—those necessary little appointments, noticed but not discussed, which contribute so much to the comfort and well-being of guests and family.

ScotTissue has made a place for itself in well-conducted homes. It is the choice of discriminating women everywhere, because of its hygienic purity and safety.

A highly-absorbent, snow-white, soothing tissue, marvelously soft as fine old linen. Kind to the most sensitive skin. Peculiarly adapted to the needs of women of intuitive daintiness. Ask your doctor.

No conversation. Just say "ScotTissue" to your storekeeper and receive a big, economical, dustproof roll.

SCOTT PAPER COMPANY, Chester, Pa.

Soft es old Linen

ScotTissue

Scott Paper Company

15 cents a roll

A 1920 magazine advertisement delicately mentions bathroom tissue (*Scott Paper Company*)

The rolls are then shipped by rail or truck to the converter, where they are cut into the desired size and transformed into familiar products. Each process is different, depending on the end product. The paper can be glued together layer upon layer until it is thick and strong, waxed until it is waterproof, and treated so it will not shrink. Or it can be fluffed into a tissue that is soft as a kitten.

Today the uses of paper are almost limitless and its consumption is expected to double by the year 2000. The colonies' first industry has now become one of our nation's greatest businesses, and it no doubt will continue to grow.

Writing paper ready for shipment (*Hammermill Paper Company*)

But the greatest contribution of paper is not industrial but the purpose for which it was first intended — for communication. Perhaps someday this communication will lead to tolerance and understanding among all peoples.

4

Watermarks, Christmas Cards, Grocery Bags and Tissues

WHEN YOU HOLD a sheet of writing paper to the light, or place it on a dark surface, you will notice an obscure design in the paper. This design is called a watermark. The watermark can be a drawing, a group of lines, an initial or words. It is a permanent part of the paper. It cannot be removed or altered, and to copy it exactly is almost impossible.

The first watermarks appeared in Fabriano, Italy, in 1282. No one seems to know for sure why they came into use. Some researchers say they were used as a trademark to identify the papermaker or the mold, or perhaps to signify the quality of the product. Others say watermarks served as the symbol of a secret brotherhood because many of the old ones were familiar religious signs such as crosses,

53

Benjamin Franklin's personal watermark

circles, triangles or fish. Or perhaps the craftsman simply was satisfying an urge to create something artistic but unobtrusive on the plain sheet of paper. Many prominent people — Benjamin Franklin, to name just one — had their own personal watermarks.

But whatever the original purpose, the watermark has played a dramatic role in the years since its introduction. In 1768 the Bank of England discovered some bank notes on which the amount of money cleverly had been increased to a larger denomination. Through the watermark the notes were traced to the papermaker, then to the purchaser, Richard William Vaughan. Vaughan was found guilty and was publicly hanged. Papermakers became even more cautious in providing watermarks that could be traced, and the populace grew so frightened that 20 years passed before there was another such incident.

In 1795 a young English lad, William Henry Ireland, forged some letters and manuscripts and claimed that William Shakespeare, the famous poet and playwright, had written them. Ireland carefully labored to copy the exact watermarks that would have been used in Shakespeare's time (a jug or a pot), and for a while he fooled many people. His collection was declared valuable. But, just before his crime was discovered, Ireland confessed his guilt, and the documents on which he had labored so long were proclaimed worthless.

Counterfeit money today can often be traced through the watermark all the way to the printer and even the date of manufacture. Many times this has led to the arrest of the counterfeiter.

Courts of law often use watermarks as evidence in verifying wills and other personal papers or in tracing forgeries. Industrial plants that manufacture vital materials for military or space projects also use watermarked paper to guard against espionage. The United States government, of course, uses the seal of the United States as its watermark.

The word *watermark*, like the name *paper*, is a

misnomer since it is not really made by water at all. Most watermarks are made by a device called a dandy roll, a hollow cylinder of wire mesh on a metal frame. While the paper is still 85 percent or more water, the wires impress a design onto the sheet, making thick and thin areas that show up only upon examination. Other watermarks are stamped onto the web of paper as it goes through the drying process. Watermarks can also be made by chemicals after the paper has left the machine.

The act of applying watermarks is considered an art and is practiced only by skilled workers.

Christmas Cards

In 1843 Sir Henry Cole, director of a museum in England, looked over a list of friends and associates to whom he should write a cheery Christmas letter — and groaned. The list was a mile long and just the thought of writing a separate letter to each made him weary.

Day after day he postponed the task until time was running out. Then he suddenly had a brilliant idea. A colorful drawing on a card could say Merry Christmas and save him all the writing!

Sir Henry hired an artist, John Calcott Horsley, and told him his plan. The artist came up with a drawing of a family gathered around a bowl of holiday punch, their cups raised in a toast to the season. Delighted, Sir Henry had 1,000 cards lithographed and handcolored and proudly mailed them out.

The cards were all but ignored.

Twenty years passed before another brave soul dared send a Christmas card — and again it was almost ignored. Then England's post office established a "penny post" rate allowing letters to be sent anywhere for a penny, and the act of sending Christmas cards inside an envelope suddenly became popular. By 1879 the postmaster general was complaining because he couldn't possibly get them all delivered before Christmas. And before 1900 rolled around, more than 200,000 different cards had been designed and printed. The first American Christmas cards were printed in 1874.

Today not only Christmas cards but birthday cards, get-well cards, congratulations and other greeting cards are a popular practice and consume large quantities of paper.

Grocery Bags

A Persian traveler on a trip to Cairo, Egypt, in 1035 was astounded to see that vegetables, spices and hardware were being wrapped in paper. It was probably the earliest example of packaging as we know it today.

In early times shoppers carried baskets to the market and packed their purchases inside. As newspapers became more abundant in the United States, grocers began wrapping fish or meat in old newspapers. They stuffed the rest of the groceries in a cheap paper cone and tied it with a string at the top. The cone, of course, was not very satisfactory because it could not be made to stand up straight.

When thick brown wrapping paper came into use, store owners required their clerks to stay after closing so they could cut squares of paper and glue three edges together to form a bag. The clerks were relieved of this duty in 1852, when Francis Wolle, a schoolteacher, invented a bagmaking machine. But the bag was flat as an envelope and could hold little. And it could not stand alone either, but had to be propped up or leaned against a wall.

Then in 1883 an ingenious idea, developed by Charles Stillwell of Philadelphia, Pennsylvania, revolutionized the grocery bag. Stillwell invented a machine to produce square-bottomed bags that could be packed full, easily carried and stood up straight. Stillwell's bag and its later improvements played a major role in the development of today's supermarkets.

Supermarkets in America now buy about 25 billion paper bags a year — 110 bags for every man, woman and child in the country, even though plastic bags for groceries are gaining in popularity.

Tissues

The boxed tissue we use for blowing our noses was not intended for nose-blowing at all. Kleenex was introduced in 1924 and called a facial tissue because it was designed for women to remove cleansing cream from their faces. A package of 100 sheets sold for 65 cents. Advertisements in newspapers and magazines showed scenes of Hollywood studios where tissues were being used by stars of the day — Helen Hayes, Elsie Janis, Gertrude Lawrence and Ronald Colman.

In 1929 the pop-up box was developed and tissues were offered in a choice of colors. But women still considered them a luxury item, reserved primarily for movie stars.

Then in 1930 a consumer test revealed some startling information. Most of the people who did buy tissues were not using them to remove cleansing cream at all. They were using them as throw-away handkerchiefs!

The idea caught on and the use of tissues soared. But during World War II the thin paper used for tissue was diverted to make insulation, industrial wipers and other products necessary for the war. Tissues virtually disappeared from the stores. When a store did receive a rare shipment, word spread rapidly and long lines formed until the last box was sold.

When the war ended tissues again appeared on the shelves in a variety of colors and in decorator packaging. Today they are used as standard equipment in practically every household, in offices, restaurant rest rooms, hotels and motels.

The late Dard Hunter, internationally known paper historian, is making paper by hand (*The Dard Hunter Paper Museum*)

5

Papermaking and You

ALTHOUGH IT HAS TAKEN 20 centuries to develop means to manufacture paper at today's speed, many artists and craftspeople still make paper by hand, just as some people choose to spin yarn or to weave fabric by hand. The paper produced by hand is used for art projects or as a luxury writing paper.

Sometimes making paper by hand is used as a classroom or a club project. If you would like to make a simple form of paper using items usually found around the house you may send for a booklet, *How To Make Paper By Hand*, by writing:

Hammermill Paper Company
Educational Services
1579 East Lake Road
Erie, Pennsylvania 16512

Enclose 25 cents for handling.

The paper you make will be recycled, since you will use paper rather than raw fibers as your organic material.

If you would like to know more about careers in the paper industry, there are many areas to explore — manufacturing, engineering, research, sales, management. Or perhaps a career in forestry.

For information, write to the following associations and request their brochures on schools and careers in the paper industry:

American Forest Institute
1619 Massachusetts Avenue N.W.
Washington, D.C. 20036

American Paper Institute
260 Madison Avenue
New York, N.Y. 10016

U.S. Forest Service, USDA
12th & Independence S.W.
Washington, D.C. 20013

Society of American Foresters
5400 Grosvenor Lane
Bethesda, Maryland 20815

Technical Association of the
Pulp & Paper Industry
One Dunwoody Park
Atlanta, Georgia 30341

 WALLIS ELEMENTARY SCHOOL

Society of Wood Science and Technology
P.O. Box 5062
Madison, Wisconsin 53705

Institute of Paper Chemistry
Appleton, Wisconsin 54912

Index